Copyright © 2000 by Nord-Süd Verlag AG, Gossau Zürich, Switzerland
First published in Switzerland under the title *Oskar der kleine Elefant*
English translation copyright © 2000 by North-South Books Inc.
All rights reserved. No part of this book may be reproduced or utilized
in any form or by any means, electronic or mechanical, including
photocopying, recording, or any information storage and retrieval
system, without permission in writing from the publisher.

First published in the United States, Great Britain, Canada,
Australia, and New Zealand in 2000 by North-South Books,
an imprint of Nord-Süd Verlag AG, Gossau Zürich, Switzerland.
Distributed in the United States by North-South Books Inc., New York.

Library of Congress Cataloging-in-Publication Data is available.
A CIP catalogue record for this book is available from The British Library.
ISBN 0-7358-1297-7 (trade binding)
1 3 5 7 9 TB 10 8 6 4 2
ISBN 0-7358-1298-5 (library binding)
1 3 5 7 9 LB 10 8 6 4 2
Printed in Belgium
For more information about our books, and the authors and artists
who create them, visit our web site: www.northsouth.com

# Little Elephant's Song

By Wolfram Hänel

Illustrated by Cristina Kadmon

*Translated by J. Alison James*

North-South Books

New York / London

On the day the little elephant was born, the first thing he had to learn was how to stand up and walk. It was not so easy, considering that he had four legs that all wanted to go in different directions. But soon he was walking between his mother and his aunts, as safe as could be.

Within a few days, his big brother and sister
had taught him some tricks. Soon he could walk
backwards, hop on three legs, and spin around
like a falling leaf.

What he liked to do best of all was dash right between his mother's great legs, back to front and front to back until she nearly lost her balance. But the little elephant's mother never got angry. She was proud of her son and all that he could do.

"Now you must learn to use your trunk," she said. "Your trunk is as important as your legs."

So the little elephant learned all he could do with a trunk. First he caught the bananas that his mother fed to him. Then he picked them himself. At last he could even pull the banana peels out of his mouth and flick them under his brother's feet so he slipped on them. The little elephant also learned how to hold onto the tail of his mother and follow along behind her. And he used his trunk to tease his sister, blowing in her ear just as she was trying to get to sleep.

But the best thing the little elephant learned
to do with his trunk was to fill it with water. First
he found he could spray a cool shower over his
back. Then he discovered it was much more fun
to sneak up on someone and spray a load of
water in his face.

The little elephant was full of mischief, but did
his mother get annoyed? No, she was pleased to
see how much he was able to do.

One day, when the father elephant and his friends came to visit, the mother said, "Just look what our baby can do! He can hop on three legs and pick bananas and spray water. I am so proud of him."

"Good, good," said his father.

But his father's friend said, "Has he learned to trumpet?"

"No," said the baby's mother. "But he is still rather young."

"I suppose so," said the friend. "But an elephant who can't trumpet is not a real elephant."

"Well then," said his father. "Give it a try, Son," and he lifted his own gigantic trunk and produced a bellowing roar that shook the banana trees.

"It really is very simple," said his mother gently. "Just like this," and she trumpeted beautifully.

"Try it!" said his sister.

"Come on," said his brother.

The little elephant didn't know what they wanted him to do. He lifted up his little trunk and blew out a thin spray of water. *Pfft!*

"Ha, ha, ha," laughed his father's friend. "That wasn't very good. He still has a lot to learn."

The mother elephant rose to her full height and glared at the visitors. "He will trumpet when he is ready," she said firmly.

The only thing the little elephant's mother was worried about was danger. Not all animals on the savannah were plant eaters, like the hippopotamus. And although full-grown elephants are strong, a little elephant is easy prey. Until her son had a good loud trumpet, he wouldn't be able to call for help.

One day the elephant family heard a high-pitched rumble down by the river, and at once they raced to the water's edge. There was the little elephant, surprised at their sudden appearance. They looked so worried, as if he were in trouble!

What's wrong? wondered the little elephant.
I just did this: And he lifted his trunk and dashed towards the shore, blowing madly. A wild, high-pitched trumpet rang out. "*Terooot!*"

His mother and aunt and brother and sister gasped in surprise.

Pleased, the little elephant did it again and again. "*Terooot! Terooot!*"

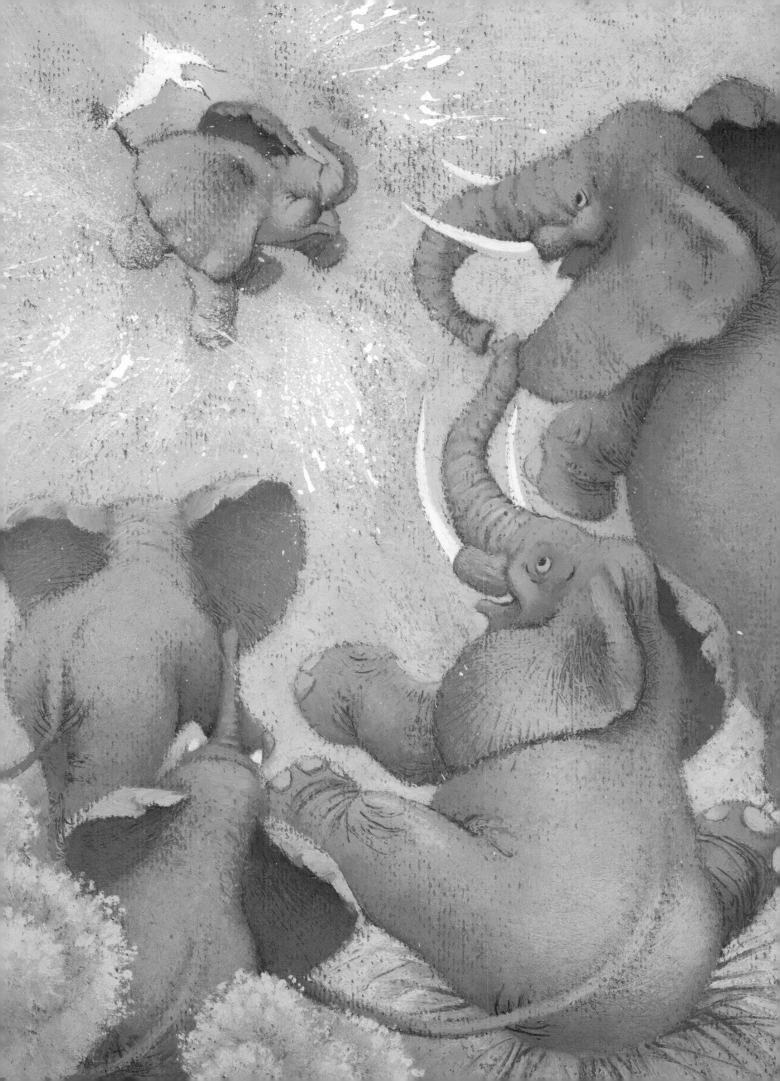

"Now *that* is how you call for help," said his mother. "We'll always be listening for you, wherever you are."

"*Terooot!*" trumpeted the little elephant quietly. It was a happy sound, because he felt good and safe right where he was.

A few days later, the elephant father and his friend were walking nearby. They heard a high-pitched trumpeting sound. "What was that?" asked the friend.

"*Ssh*," said the father. "It sounded like my son." But they heard nothing more, for the happy little elephant was busy learning how to turn somersaults!

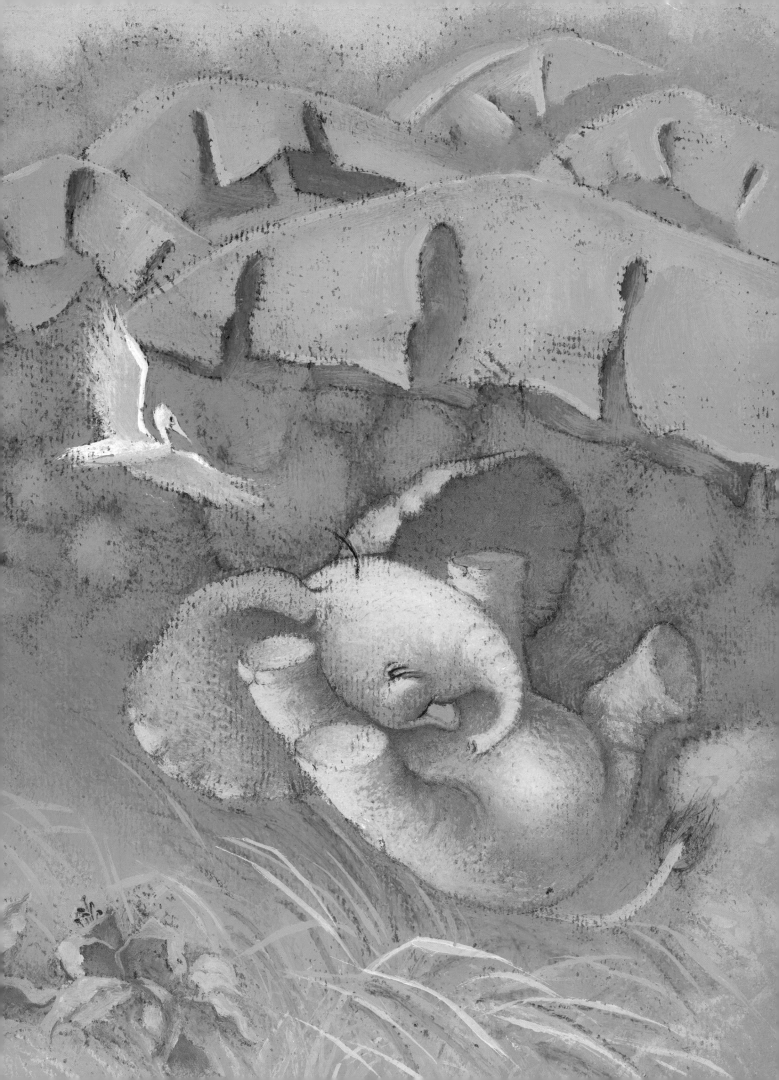